The Winners series brings you exciting sports stories for girls about girls. Step inside the worlds of figure skating, horseback riding, soccer, and softball and see what it takes to be a true champion. Winners isn't just great reading—it's a fantastic way to learn about different sports, about relationships, and about faith in God.

Books by Linda Lee Maifair

Darcy J. Doyle, Daring Detective

The Case of the Angry Actress
The Case of the Bashed-Up Bicycle
The Case of the Bashful Bully
The Case of the Choosey Cheater
The Case of the Creepy Campout
The Case of the Giggling Ghost
The Case of the Missing Max
The Case of the Mixed-Up Monsters
The Case of the Nearsighted Neighbors
The Case of the Pampered Poodle
The Case of the Sweet-Toothed Shoplifter
The Case of the Troublesome Treasure

Winners

Batter Up, Bailey Benson!
Go Figure, Gabriella Grant!
Use Your Head, Molly Malone!
Whoa There, Wanda Wilson!

Linda Lee Maifair

Whoa There, Wanda Wilson!

ZondervanPublishingHouse
Grand Rapids, Michigan

A Division of HarperCollins*Publishers*

Whoa There, Wanda Wilson!

Copyright © 1997 by Linda Lee Maifair

Requests for information should be addressed to:

ZondervanPublishingHouse
Grand Rapids, Michigan 49530

ISBN 0-310-20703-7

Interior illustrations by Gloria Oostema

Printed in the United States of America

97 98 99 00 01 02 03 04 /❖ DC/ 10 9 8 7 6 5 4 3 2 1

For Marguerite and Leslie

Chapter One

Wanda Wilson loved horses. She loved reading about horses. She loved riding horses. She loved competing in horse shows. She loved all the horse grooming and the tack polishing that went with it. She especially loved having her own horse, Gypsy Lady. The only thing Wanda *didn't* like was the daily chore of mucking out stalls.

Wanda thought *muck*—a cross between *mud* and *yuck*—was a good name for it. And since she worked part-time at Apple Valley Stables, Wanda saw a lot of it. By the time she got around to Gypsy's stall, she usually finished the job as quickly as she could. She could clean up the droppings, gather up the wet and soiled straw, turn over the straw that was left, put down new bedding, and haul the dirty stuff away to the muck pile in fifteen minutes flat.

But today was different. There was a new girl coming to the stables all the way from Colorado. Tara Bradwell, President of the Apple Valley Riding Club, had asked Wanda to "check her out" since Tara couldn't be there herself.

Ordered was more like it. "See what she's like," Tara had instructed. "You know, be my spy. Wheedle as much information as you can out of her. Then report back to me!"

Wanda hadn't much liked the idea of spying, and she was way too shy to be very good at wheedling. But she didn't quite know how to tell that to Tara. So there she was, taking her time, stretching out the mucking and raking and hauling to be sure she'd still be there to "check out" the new girl when she finally arrived. Gypsy's stall had never been mucked out so well!

Wanda had just turned the same clump of straw for what seemed like the hundredth time when an old pickup truck hauling a horse trailer pulled into the yard. And she just happened to be wheeling her last wheelbarrow load to the muck pile when Melissa Barnes, the stable owner, was directing the driver to the parking area closest to the barn. Her timing was perfect.

"Wanda!" Melissa called to her. "Come on over and meet our new boarders!"

A tall, gangly, blonde-haired girl hopped down from the passenger side of the truck cab as Wanda walked over to the trailer.

"Whooee!" the girl said loudly, rubbing her rear with the palms of both hands. "My backside's so numb, I don't even want to *think* about sitting for a month!" Wanda, who never would have done or said such a thing, couldn't help but giggle.

Melissa Barnes laughed, too, as she introduced them. "Cheree Davenport," she said to the new girl, "this is Wanda Wilson." She nodded in Wanda's direction. "Wanda's a member of the riding club I was telling you about, and you'll be boarding your horse next to hers. Wanda, why don't you show Cheree around while Mr. Davenport and I go in and take care of some paperwork?"

Melissa and Mr. Davenport walked to the tack building where Melissa kept her stable office, leaving the two girls in the yard. It would have been a good chance to start "checking out" the new girl, but Wanda had no idea where to start. She didn't even know how to begin a conversation.

Cheree took care of that. "Hey there, Wanda!" she said, grinning broadly. "How ya doin'?"

Wanda usually found it hard to talk to new people, even people her own age, but Cheree's friendly smile was contagious. "Hi," she said, returning the grin. She wished she could think of something else to say or do.

"How 'bout helping me get Clancy out of the trailer?" Cheree asked. "He's going to be spittin' mad if I keep him in there much longer."

"Sure," Wanda said, glad to have something to do instead of having to think of something to say. Together the girls unlatched the back of the horse trailer, opened the door, and let down the loading ramp. "Wow!" Wanda said when she saw the big gray-and-white spotted horse inside. "An Appaloosa?"

Cheree nodded. "He's somethin', isn't he?" she said proudly.

None of the girls in the Apple Valley Riding Club had an Appaloosa, and Wanda had never seen one at any of the local English riding competitions she'd been to, either. She wondered what Tara Bradwell would think about it. "He's gorgeous," she told Cheree.

"Shhhh!" Cheree said, giving her a wink. "Don't let him hear you say that. He thinks too much of himself already!"

The horse snorted in greeting and pawed impatiently at the floor as Cheree climbed up into the trailer. Cheree rubbed her fingertips under his chin, then scratched behind his ears, just the way Wanda always did with Gypsy. "You're tired of this old trailer, aren't you?" Cheree told him. Clancy snorted again as Cheree clipped a lead line to his halter, put a hand on his shoulder, and urged him backward down the ramp to where Wanda was waiting.

Both the girl and the horse looked friendly enough, but Wanda just stood there, still not knowing what to do or say.

Cheree took care of that, too. "If you've got any treats on you," she said, "he'll be your friend for life."

Wanda laughed. She always had a few chunks of apple or carrot slices or sugar cubes in her pockets for Gypsy and the other horses in the boarding barn. She put an apple wedge in her open palm and held it out to the horse. Clancy stretched out his neck and snuffled at the offering for a few seconds before nibbling it from her hand, his muzzle wet and his breath warm against her skin. He munched in noisy, closed-eyed happiness for a few seconds. Then he moved closer to sniffle at Wanda's treat pocket, giving her a gentle nudge to let her know what he wanted.

"Whoa there, Clancy Boy!" Cheree told him, pulling him back. "You better mind your manners!"

"It's okay," Wanda said, laughing. She reached into her pocket and gave the horse another chunk of fruit.

"He must be 'bout ready to jump out of his skin," Cheree said. She looked around the grounds. "Is there someplace I can let him run a little before I get him bedded down?"

Wanda nodded. "The paddock behind the barn."

She led the way over, held the gate open while Cheree led Clancy inside, then shut the gate behind her again when Cheree came out.

Clancy acted just like a little kid let loose after a long day at school. His dark tail billowing out behind him, he galloped up and down the length of the small, fenced-in pasture. He'd swoop over to where Cheree and Wanda stood by the rail watching him, then gallop off again before they could pat him, tossing his head in mischievous joy.

Clancy finally settled down enough to start sampling the grass, and Wanda nervously asked Cheree if she wanted to see the rest of the stable grounds.

"You bet! But hold on a second there, Wanda," Cheree said, agreeably. She walked over to the pickup truck and reached inside the passenger door. She pulled out a wide-brimmed cowgirl hat, plopped it on her head, and strode back to where Wanda stood waiting for her.

Wanda felt herself staring at the big beige hat. None of the girls in the Apple Valley Riding Club had hats like that. She couldn't even *imagine* Tara Bradwell's wearing one. Just thinking about what

Tara might say about it left Wanda even more speechless than usual.

"Well, I'm all ready for the grand tour!" Cheree said. "If it's not too much trouble."

"Uh, no. No trouble at all." Wanda forced herself to look down, away from the hat. Just then she noticed Cheree's necklace. "Your cross is really pretty," she said. "I've never seen one like that."

Cheree held it out so Wanda could have a closer look. "It's mother-of-pearl," she said. "My grandmother got it when she was my age, and she gave it to me when I was confirmed."

Wanda pulled her own silver cross out from under her shirt where she'd been wearing it since Tara Bradwell made dumb jokes about it at an Apple Valley Riding Club meeting. "I got mine from my mother."

Cheree whistled in admiration. "That's a pretty one," she said.

"Thanks," Wanda said, wishing she was bold enough to wear it the way Cheree wore her cross—*and* her hat. She tucked the cross back under her clothes. "How about that grand tour?" she said.

Chapter Two

Wanda was afraid it would be a dull, quiet tour with her leading it, but Cheree didn't leave any room for awkward silences.

"My dad's going to teach at the seminary in the fall," Cheree told Wanda on the way to the exercise and show ring. "My mom's a preschool teacher, but she's home now with my baby brother, Willie. We left them off at the house we're rentin' on Middle Street before we came on out here with Clancy. I don't have any other brothers or sisters, but I wish I did. How 'bout you?"

Wanda was amazed that anybody could find so much to say, especially to someone she'd just met. Even more amazing, she found herself telling Cheree all about her dad's work with the National Park Service, and her mother's part-time job at PNC Bank, and the old house they had moved into two years ago. "I have *three* older brothers," she said, "and I'll be glad to loan them to you any time you want!" Cheree laughed a loud, hearty laugh at the joke, and Wanda found herself joining in.

Cheree started chatting away again. "I'm going to be in sixth grade. My best subjects are phys ed and math, but my favorite subject is lunch," she said while they inspected the big barn where Melissa kept her own horses. She laughed her contagious laugh again. "I'm especially good at spaghetti and cheeseburgers. How 'bout you?"

"I'm going to be in sixth grade, too!" Wanda told her. She admitted something she hadn't told anyone else. "I'm a little scared about going to middle school. My best subject is English." She shared another secret. "And someday I'd like to write horse books like *The Black Stallion* or *Misty*." Cheree nodded her approval, and smiled a big smile at Wanda.

"Whooee!" Cheree said when Wanda showed her the room where the Apple Valley Riding Club held its weekly meetings. "Look at all the ribbons and trophies!"

Dozens of colored ribbons and shiny trophies were arranged in separate displays, one for each member of the club. Wanda pointed to the biggest display, right in the center, the one with the most blue ribbons and championship awards. "These are Tara Bradwell's," she said. "She's president of our riding club and our best rider."

"Hmmm. Where's yours?" Cheree asked Wanda.

Wanda was flattered that she'd asked, and a little embarrassed to show her. "Over here," she said, walking over to the smallest display where the few ribbons were all yellow and white. "I'm just starting out," she explained. "Until I joined the riding club a couple of months ago, I was way too nervous to do any competing."

Cheree gave her a warm, encouraging smile. "Looks to me like you're doin' right well!" she said.

Wanda smiled back at her. "Do you ride in competitions?" she asked as she led the way to the smaller barn where Gypsy and Clancy would be boarding together.

Cheree stopped and tipped her hat back on her head. "I like to," she said with a sigh. "But with the move and all, I haven't been able to do much lately."

Wanda knew what to do about *that*. "Then you've got to come to the show this weekend in Littlestown!" she told Cheree. "It's not far, and our whole riding club is going. Melissa is taking me and Gypsy in one of her big trailers. You can come with us!"

Cheree smiled. "That sounds like fun!" she said. She stopped in her tracks when Wanda opened the door to the boarding barn and led the way inside. "Well, would you look at this!" she said. "Old Clancy is going to love it here!"

Wanda nodded. The stalls were roomy and clean, and the barn itself was bright and airy and smelled of fresh hay. "Gypsy likes it a lot."

A half dozen horses nickered, whinnied, or snorted for attention when the girls entered the stable. As they passed down the line of stalls, Wanda introduced Cheree to each horse, telling her a little bit about each animal's habits and temperament.

"This is Aladdin," she said at the first stall. She

offered a bit of apple to the big gray Arabian. "Beth Ann Gibbon's horse."

"Hey there, Aladdin!" Cheree said, giving him a pat and a smile.

"He tries to act big and brave," Wanda said. "But a baby rabbit got into the barn last week and scooted by his stall, and we almost had to peel Aladdin off the ceiling!"

Cheree giggled.

Two doors down was a jet-black Morgan. "This is Amanda Riggles' horse," Wanda said as she offered the mare a sugar cube. "She has a long, fancy name, but Amanda just calls her Giggles." As if on cue, the horse bared her teeth in a horsey grin and snorted in loud, horsey laughter.

Cheree joined in, her laughter much the same. "I can see why," she said.

When they came to the only double-sized stall, the sleek chestnut quarterhorse inside didn't meet them at the door as the others had done. Wanda had to reach way out over the top of the railing before the mare would take the sugar cube she was offered.

Wanda gave the horse a deep bow, like a loyal subject greeting royalty. "This is Abbington Acres Royal Wildemere Majesty," she told Cheree. "And she thinks she's the queen of the stable."

"Whooee," said Wanda as she peered over the door at the animal's fancy royal-blue stable blanket. "And doesn't she just look it, too?" she said. She read the monogram on the blanket. "T.A.B.?" she asked.

Wanda made a face. "Tara Alexis Bradwell," she said. "The *real* queen of Apple Valley Stables."

If Cheree noticed the sour face or the sarcastic tone to Wanda's voice, she didn't say anything. "You sure know a lot about these horses," she said.

"I work here," Wanda said, a little embarrassed to tell Cheree. "So I see a lot of them." She saw a lot of currycombs, feed buckets, and muck piles, too, but she didn't tell Cheree about that.

"Now that's what I call a great job!" Cheree said, smacking her cowgirl hat against her thigh.

"Really?" Wanda said, surprised. Tara Bradwell always made her feel like she was some kind of stable servant.

21

"Sure!" Cheree said. "Working around all these great horses all the time and getting paid for it, to boot! What could be better than that?" She paused. "What about the other girls in the riding club?" she asked.

"Oh, *they* don't work here," Wanda said. "They just board their horses, or take their riding lessons with Melissa."

Cheree shook her head. "No, I mean what are the other girls like?"

Wanda blushed. She didn't really know all that much about the other girls. Horses were a whole lot easier for her to talk to than people, and at meetings, Tara Bradwell did most of the talking anyway. She shrugged. "I've only been in the club for a couple of months," she said.

"This is where Gypsy stays," Wanda announced as they reached her stall.

"You sure do keep it tidy," Cheree told her.

Wanda blushed again, not wanting to tell Cheree exactly *why* the stall was so tidy today. She pointed out the freshly bedded stall at the end of the line. "And here's the one Melissa and I got ready for

Clancy, right next door," she said. "Gypsy will be happy to have a new neighbor."

"Where *is* Gypsy?" Cheree asked.

"Out back," Wanda said. She eagerly led the way to the rear of the barn, anxious to show off her pretty bay mare. As they neared the back of the barn, Wanda smiled sheepishly at Cheree and then gave a loud whistle.

Gypsy was right there waiting for her when she opened the door—grinning and whinnying and covered with fresh mud from forelock to flank. She had found what had to be the only mud puddle in Adams County and rolled in it, more than once by the looks of her. Wanda felt her face flush with embarrassment.

"Gypsy Chesapeake Bay Lady!" she scolded, using the horse's full name the way her parents used "Wanda Lynn Wilson" when they were angry with her. "Just look at you! How could you be so—"

Cheree laughed her loud, hearty laugh. "Whoa there, Wanda Wilson," she said. "Don't you be too hard on her now." She reached into her pocket and pulled out a sugar cube and offered it to the mare.

She ran a gentle hand down across the horse's mud-splattered withers and back. "What a dainty beauty you are," she said softly, and Gypsy nickered in reply.

"What a *dirty* beauty she is," Wanda corrected.

Cheree laughed. "I remember once when we were ready to ride in the Tri-County Junior Western Championships and Clancy found a doozy of a mud puddle. Was *he* ever a mess!"

"*Western* Championships?" Wanda said, even though she'd sort of figured that out already. None of the girls at the Apple Valley Riding Club rode Western, and at mixed competitions, Tara Bradwell always made fun of those who did. The same Tara Bradwell who would be calling her at six-thirty sharp to get her report on Cheree.

Chapter Three

Tara Bradwell congratulated Wanda on her snooping and wheedling when Wanda told her about Cheree Davenport, her family, her horse Clancy, and even her favorite foods and subjects in school.

"I didn't think you'd find out *anything*!" Tara told her. "I told Beth Ann and the other girls you'd probably just stand there with your mouth shut as usual."

The comment about her shyness hurt Wanda's feelings, but, as usual, she kept her mouth shut and didn't say anything.

"So," Tara said. "You think she'll fit in at the Apple Valley Riding Club?"

Wanda hadn't told Tara that Wanda was a Western rider. *What difference should that make?* she told herself. *We all ride and we all love horses.* "Sure," she said. "Why not?"

"Well, you know," Tara reminded her, "Apple Valley has a reputation to keep up. We're the number-one riding club in Adams County and the whole South Central District! We can't let just *anybody* join."

That remark hurt Wanda's feelings, too. Apple Valley *was* the top riding club in Adams County and the whole South Central District, and Wanda was glad to be a part of it, but sometimes Tara made her feel as if she didn't fit in, either.

"She's nice," Wanda told Tara about Cheree. "You'll like her."

"We'll see," Tara said. "What time will she be at the stables tomorrow? I want to check her out for myself."

Wanda hesitated. She didn't want to help Tara check out anybody anymore.

"Helloooo?" Tara said sarcastically, as if Wanda was being really dense and not paying enough atten-

26

tion. "What time is this girl going to be at the stables tomorrow?"

Wanda sighed. Tara Bradwell was confident and outspoken and pushy. Even over the phone, Wanda had trouble standing up to her. "About noon, I think," she said. "But . . ."

"I'll be there!" Tara said. She hung up without thanking Wanda or even saying good-bye.

Wanda made sure that she was at the stables about noon the next day, too. She had no idea what she could do about it, but she had a bad feeling about Tara's meeting Cheree.

Cheree was riding Clancy out in the exercise ring when she got there. She took off her wide-brimmed cowgirl hat and waved it at Wanda when she saw her. "Hey there, Wanda Wilson!" she hollered. "Watch this!"

She moved Clancy from a walk to a jog to a lope, making it look smooth and easy. Then she let out a whoop and charged at the row of trash cans and flowerpots lined up like racing barrels, several feet

apart in the middle of the ring. Still whooping and hollering, she galloped full tilt toward the first can, reining in just enough to maneuver in a fast, tight circle around it without brushing against it or knocking it over. Then she urged Clancy on toward the flowerpot ahead of it and did the same thing.

Cheree and Clancy moved as a unit, strong and agile and confident. The horse and rider leaned way into the turns, this way, that way, making pivots and circles that Wanda never would have dared to make on Gypsy. At that speed, she would have fallen off the saddle or turned the horse over. Wanda was so fascinated watching Cheree move Clancy in and out and around the obstacles that at first she didn't even notice that Tara Bradwell had arrived and had come over to stand beside her at the rail.

"Whooee!" Cheree yelled when the ride was done. She waved her hat at Wanda again before slowing Clancy to a walk so he could cool down.

Wanda felt Tara's eyes on her, and she stared straight ahead at Clancy and Cheree.

"That *can't* be the new girl," Tara said.

Wanda stared at the newly painted fence rail in front of her.

"You know, the one you checked out for me?" Tara went on. "The one you said was Apple Valley Riding Club material?"

Wanda stared at the meadow way beyond the riding ring.

Tara tapped her sharply on the shoulder. "Hellooo?" she said. She nodded toward Cheree and Clancy, still walking around the ring. "That can't be the Cheree Davenport you told me about," she said.

Wanda smiled weakly. "She's really a good rider, isn't she?"

"A good rider?" Tara said, astonished.

Wanda worked up the courage to argue the point. "No, really," she said. "She's good. Didn't you see the way she rode—"

"That wasn't riding!" Tara said. "That was . . . that was . . ." She scrunched up her face as if she was trying to think of a word bad enough to describe it.

"Exciting?" Wanda dared to suggest. Just watching had made her breathless.

"Dumb!" Tara said. She wrinkled up her nose as

if she were standing too close to the muck pile. "And what's with those clothes!"

Wanda looked at Cheree's hat, plaid flannel shirt, faded jeans, and cowboy boots. She thought it was a good outfit for practice riding, kind of neat and comfortable. "It suits the kind of riding she does," she told Tara. "Just like our English riding out-fits suit—" She stopped in midsentence. Cheree had dismounted and was leading Clancy over toward them.

Cheree gave both girls a big smile. "Hey there!" she said.

Wanda felt a knot forming in the pit of her stomach as the distance between Tara and Cheree got smaller. The knot pulled into a tight, hard lump when Tara leaned over and whispered in Wanda's ear. *"You've got to be kidding!"* she said.

Chapter Four

Even though she dreaded doing it, Wanda introduced them. "This is Tara Bradwell," she told Cheree.

Cheree grinned. "Whooee!" she said. "The one with all those awards?"

Tara smiled a thin smile. "Yes," she said. "*Thirty-nine* blue ribbons and *fourteen* championship trophies."

"Wow!" Cheree said. "That's a lot."

Tara smiled her thin smile again. "How many do *you* have?" she asked Cheree.

Cheree laughed her loud, hearty laugh. "Oh, I don't keep count!" she said, as if she thought it was a sort of silly thing to do. "A couple of boxes full."

Tara and Wanda's eyes widened. "You can go right ahead and count them if you want when I bring them in next week."

Tara's eyes widened even further. "Bring them in where?" she asked.

Cheree took off her hat and mopped her brow with the back of one plaid flannel sleeve. She used the hat to point to the building where the Apple Valley Riding Club had its meetings. "To your club room," she said. "Wanda says I should bring them in when I come to my first meeting. She says all the members keep their ribbons and stuff here."

Tara glared at Wanda.

Wanda stared at Cheree's cowgirl boots. They were really nice, she thought. Much fancier than the tall black boots she wore when she rode in English competition.

"I didn't think we'd be ready for this weekend," Cheree went on. She patted Clancy on the shoulder. "But old Clancy here did real well this morning, and he enjoyed it, so I think I'll go after all."

Wanda could feel Tara's eyes boring down on her again. She went from studying Cheree's boots to studying Clancy's front hooves not far behind them. They had the Appaloosa stripes that Wanda had read about in one of her horse books. And Cheree took good care of them, she noticed, keeping them trimmed and clean, just the way she did for Gypsy.

"Go where?" Tara asked Cheree.

"To that competition you're all going to. In Littlestown, is it?"

"It's not a *rodeo*," Tara was quick to point out.

"Yeah, I know," Cheree said. "But Wanda says there will be some Western classes I can enter."

Tara glared at Wanda again.

"Come on, I'll go in with you," Wanda said quickly to Cheree, even though Cheree hadn't said anything about leaving. She opened the gate to let Clancy and Cheree out of the ring. "I have to start cleaning the stalls." She had never felt so anxious to get a pitchfork full of muck in her hands.

Tara Bradwell had other ideas. She grabbed Wanda by the wrist. "Not yet," she said, holding her arm way too tight. "I need to talk to you for a minute first."

Cheree smiled at Wanda. "You just stay and finish

talkin' to your friend," she said. "Me and Clancy'll be in the barn." She led the horse out of the gate and across the yard toward the boarding stable.

Cheree and Clancy were barely out of earshot when Tara turned on Wanda. "You've *got* to be kidding!" she said again.

"About what?" Wanda asked, though she had a pretty good idea already.

"Her!" Tara said, waving a hand in Cheree's direction. "That ... that *cowgirl!* And her shaggy horse. And her trash cans and flowerpots and her 'Whooee'!"

Wanda managed to look her in the eye. "Clancy isn't shaggy," she said. "And they don't use flowerpots and trash cans in competitions. She was just ..."

"You know what I mean!" Tara interrupted. "She's not like the rest of us. She doesn't fit in."

Wanda's felt her face get hot. But before she could think of some protest or work up the nerve to say it, Tara went on. "*You* invited her to join the club and go to the competition, so you'll just have to *un*invite her," she said. She turned on her heel and started walking away.

Wanda surprised both of them when she reached out and grabbed Tara's arm. "There's nothing wrong with Cheree Davenport!" she said. She felt her confidence drain away in the face of Tara's angry, unwavering glare. "B–besides," she stammered, "Melissa told her about the club before she even moved here. And Melissa already said she'd give her a ride to the competition, so we can't uninvite her now."

Tara's glare turned into a smirk. "Fine," she said. "But if I were you, and I wanted to stay in the Apple Valley Riding Club, I'd make sure that cowgirl doesn't embarrass us on Saturday." She turned and stomped away, leaving Wanda standing in her dust.

Chapter Five

On Saturday morning, when Cheree tried to lead Clancy onto the horse trailer to go to the competition, the Appaloosa didn't want to go. He shook his head. He pawed and snorted. He dragged her backward away from it. When Cheree tried leading him up to the ramp for the second time, he reared and pawed and snorted some more.

"Whoa, Clancy!" Cheree told him. "What's got into you?"

"He probably thinks you're moving again," Wanda suggested. "Let's put Gypsy on first and see what happens."

They tethered the Appaloosa near the trailer and went back to the barn for the bay. She nickered at

Clancy on her way past him, and he whinnied back. When Gypsy walked up into the trailer without a problem, Clancy pulled at his tether line, anxious to go along for the ride.

"Whooee!" Cheree exclaimed as she led the eager horse up into the trailer behind the mare. "You're a genius, Wanda!"

Wanda wished it were true. If she were really a genius she'd know what to do about getting Cheree to stop saying things like "Whooee!" when Tara and the others were around.

"I just know how much they like each other already," she said.

Cheree grinned. "Sort of like me and you, hey?"

Wanda did like Cheree already, just the way she was. She knew she shouldn't even be *thinking* about trying to change her to suit Tara Bradwell and the Apple Valley Riding Club. "Yeah," she said, quietly fingering the silver chain of her necklace. "Just like me and you."

They helped Melissa load her own horse onto the trailer, then they sat side by side in the cab and chatted nonstop all the way to the competition.

"Wanda!" Melissa said with obvious pleasure. "I don't think I've ever heard you say so much!"

Cheree grinned. "My dad says I started talking when I was five months old and haven't stopped to take a deep breath since!" She laughed her big hearty laugh. "I guess it's catching!"

Even though Wanda wished she could think of some way to get her to tone the laugh down a little when they got to Littlestown, she couldn't help but join in. "It just helps to have somebody who's easy to talk to," she said, and Cheree smiled.

When they got to the show grounds, Melissa parked in a big, open field with dozens of other trailers. Wanda and Cheree got their horses out and tethered them nearby while they unloaded their gear. They finished their last-minute grooming and tacking-up chores, then got dressed for their competitions.

Wanda was already wearing her white turtleneck, white stretch breeches, and tall black riding boots. She put on a black jacket and a matching hard "hunter's" riding cap, cinching the strap taut under her chin. "Let's go check the schedule," she said to Cheree.

Cheree laughed. "Whoa there, Wanda Wilson!" she said. "Hold your horses. I'm only half ready!"

Wanda looked at Cheree's bright teal, fancy-fringed shirt, matching teal pants, and elaborately tooled cowgirl boots. She could only guess what Tara Bradwell would think of *that* outfit. She was almost afraid to find out what else Cheree was planning to put on.

Cheree pulled a brightly embroidered lavender vest and a cowgirl hat out of a big paper bag. It was not the usual beige felt hat Wanda was used to seeing her wear. This hat was the same bright teal as Cheree's shirt and pants and had three brightly dyed fuchsia feathers stuck in its wide lavender band. She slipped on the vest and put on the hat at a jaunty angle. "*Now* I'm ready," she told Wanda. "What do you think?"

Wanda thought Cheree's outfit was bright and pretty. Fun, just like Cheree. But she could just imagine what Tara Bradwell, whom she saw getting ready for her own ride outside her fancy trailer not far away, would have to say about it. "People at these shows don't usually dress so … so …" She struggled to come up with the right word, one that wouldn't hurt Cheree's feelings. "So *colorfully*," she said.

Cheree laughed her loud, hearty laugh. "Yeah, I can see that," she said, waving a hand at the parking and showing areas around her before she put it on. "We're practically up to our eyeballs in dark jackets, black boots, and little dark hats!" She grinned at Wanda's plain dark jacket, black boots, and little dark hat. "Good thing there are a couple of Western riders here today to liven things up a little for you English people!" She regarded her own outfit with a wide smile. "Think the judges will notice me in this?"

"I think you'll be hard to ignore," Wanda told her, which was exactly the trouble in the first place. It set off another roll of Cheree's equally hard-to-ignore laughter, making Wanda glance nervously over toward Tara's trailer to see if she'd noticed. The scowl on Tara's face told her all too clearly that Tara had.

Cheree glanced over in the same direction. "Hey, there, Tara Bradwell!" she hollered.

She took off her teal, lavender, and fuchsia hat and waved it in a wide arc back and forth over her head.

Tara nodded curtly, then turned around, pretending to be busy braiding her horse's mane and tail, English style. Wanda could imagine what she was thinking. "Uh, maybe we'd better keep it down a little," she told Cheree. "You know, the laughing and the hollering, so we don't spook the horses."

Cheree was agreeable, as usual. "Want to go over there and talk to her?" she suggested. "Or maybe you could take me around to meet some of the other girls in the club?"

Cheree sounded anxious to do it, but it was the last thing Wanda wanted to do: meet more girls like Tara who would be just as bad as she was. "Uh, no," she said, fumbling to find an excuse. "We better not. Your class runs first, so you better get Clancy over to the ring."

Wanda went with her as Cheree walked Clancy to the competition area. She wished she could find someplace big enough to hide two girls and a large, spotted horse, when she saw Tara Bradwell and Beth Ann Gibbons headed in their direction.

Tara and Beth Ann were wearing expensive, matching riding outfits. With their hair done up exactly the same way, they looked almost like twins. *Just what I need*, Wanda thought. *TWO of them to worry about!*

Cheree didn't seem worried at all. "How ya doin'?" she asked Tara.

Tara looked like she had just swallowed a lemon or had a piece of Limburger cheese up her nose. She nodded curtly again and introduced Beth Ann. "This is Cheree," she said. "The girl I've been telling you so much about."

Beth Ann looked Cheree up and down, and for a second or two Wanda thought she was going to say something rude the way Tara might do. Beth Ann surprised her. "Wow!" she said to Cheree. "I really like your outfit!" Tara shot Beth Ann a scathing look.

Cheree smiled. "Thanks," she said. "Wanda here thought I might be goin' a little overboard."

Wanda's face flushed. She didn't really think that at all, and she was embarrassed and annoyed that she'd let Tara bully her into making Cheree think she did.

Beth Ann patted Clancy on the shoulder. "Nice horse, too!" she said.

Tara looked like she was ready to spit.

"And I *like* that saddle!" Beth Ann said.

It was too much for Tara. "Too bad you need a handle to stay on," she said, referring to the fact that Cheree's Western saddle had a saddle horn and English saddles didn't.

"Sometimes when I'm pole bending or barrel racing and I go too fast or get too cocky, even the handle isn't enough to keep me on!" Cheree said good-naturedly. Beth Ann chuckled until Tara poked her in the ribs. Cheree clapped a hand over her own mouth, mid-chortle. "Sorry," Cheree said. "Wanda says I need to keep it down some."

Wanda blushed again, but the announcer's call for the first Western class took away any chance she had to say or do anything about it.

"That's me," Cheree said, her eyes full of anticipation. "Don't you forget to watch and cheer me on, now."

"Believe me," Tara said, "we wouldn't miss it for anything."

Tara's sarcastic tone made Wanda really angry. She imagined herself opening her mouth and saying,

The last thing I want to do is stand at the rail with you, Tara Bradwell, listening to your snide remarks about Cheree Davenport and Clancy.

But Tara turned and arched one eyebrow at her, and Wanda stood there, fiddling with her cross necklace, and didn't say a thing.

Chapter Six

They all stood at the fence rail—Tara, Beth Ann, and Wanda—as Cheree rode into the ring with two other Western riders.

Wanda watched Cheree's riding technique. Her posture in the saddle. The position of her hands on the reins. The way she moved through the gaits at the announcer's command, smoothly changing from walk to jog to lope, moving clockwise around the ring, then counterclockwise, around and through the shrubs and posts that marked the course. Cheree looked confident and in control. She and Clancy made an impressive pair.

"She's better than the other two," Wanda said aloud. "She should get first place."

Tara rolled her eyes. "How hard is it to place first when there are only three riders?" she said. "My smallest class today has eleven!" She looked expectantly from Wanda to Beth Ann, as if waiting for them to agree with her. They didn't.

"Oh, brother," Tara said sarcastically, when Cheree and the other riders went back to the lope. "Yippi-ti-yi-yay!"

"You know," Wanda said, working up her courage to confront Tara. "It's not really all that different from our riding."

Tara raised one eyebrow and gave Wanda a disgusted shake of the head as if she felt really sorry for anybody who could be so dumb.

As usual, it shook Wanda's confidence. "I mean, besides the clothes. And some of the tack. And the riding techniques," she struggled to explain.

"Besides the clothes and the tack and the riding techniques?" Tara rolled her eyes. "Hellooo?" she said. "What else *is* there?"

Wanda was surprised when Beth Ann jumped into the conversation. "Well, English riders have to follow a course, too," she said. "We change gaits, just like they're doing, only we go from a walk to a trot to a canter. We're all judged on the same sort of equitation skills. How we sit a horse, control, things like that. You know, horsemanship."

"Humph!" Tara said. "All she's doing is bouncing around in some ridiculous outfit! You can't compare that to *real* riding!"

The riders in the ring were now lining up in front of the judges, where they were asked to turn and back up their horses.

"See, we do that, too," Beth Ann dared to add, and Tara humphed her into silence again.

Wanda held her breath when it was time for the winners to be announced. She felt like letting out a loud "Whooee!" when Cheree was awarded first place.

Cheree rode over to the rail and handed Wanda her new ribbon to hold while she stayed in the ring for the second Western class that was about to start.

Wanda said, "Way to go, Cheree!"

Beth Ann said, "Congratulations!"

Tara said, "Humph!" And she stood there finding fault with everything Cheree and Clancy did when they went back out into the ring.

Wanda was tired of hearing it, and tired of being too timid to speak up for her new friend. When Cheree won first place in her second event, too, Wanda turned to Tara. "I *told* you she was good!" she said.

Tara's face turned pink.

"Pretty soon she'll need a bigger display space back at the club room than you have!" Beth Ann added.

Tara's pink face turned cherry red. "I'm going to call an emergency meeting of the Apple Valley Riding Club!" she said. "Monday night. I've got a new resolution I think we should pass."

Beth Ann didn't ask. And seeing Tara's narrowed, determined eyes, Wanda was sort of afraid to. She cleared her throat and forced out the question. "What resolution?" she asked.

"The resolution to make Apple Valley an English-only riding club!" Tara said. She glowered at Beth Ann, as if she was daring her to say anything. Beth Ann didn't. Tara turned her glare on Wanda.

This time Wanda couldn't just stand there and be

quiet about it. "You can't do that!" she protested. "I won't let you!"

Tara laughed at the idea of Wanda Wilson's stopping her from doing anything. She smiled her thin smile and leaned forward, her face close to Wanda's. "Fine," she said. "But remember, I'm the president of the club. And the best rider. I'm the one everybody listens to and follows. *You're* the girl who helps out in the stable. When we vote, whose side do you think everybody will be on?"

She grabbed Beth Ann by the wrist and stomped away, right past Cheree and Clancy and the second blue ribbon now decorating Clancy's bridle. Beth Ann looked like a little kid whose mother was dragging her away from the playground to go home and take a bath. "Congratulations!" she managed to call back over her shoulder before Tara gave her arm another yank and dragged her away.

"You know," Cheree said when she'd dismounted. "I don't think that Tara Bradwell likes me very much, though I can't really figure why."

Wanda was mad. "She doesn't like you because you ride different and talk different and dress different and you aren't just like her!" she said. "Because she's snobby and jealous and mean and she's always judging people by all the wrong things!"

The more she thought about it, the angrier she got. "We should tie her martingales and lead lines and reins into one big knot! We should put boot black on her grooming brushes! We should put superglue on her saddle! We should—"

Cheree laughed her easy, hearty laugh. "Whoa there, Wanda Wilson!" she said. "Maybe you better tell me what's got you so riled up!"

"Tara wants to make the club all-English," she blurted. She didn't say exactly why, but it wasn't hard for Cheree to figure out.

"Oh," Cheree said. Then she looked doubtfully at Wanda. "If that's what you all want."

"It's not what I want!" Wanda said.

Cheree smiled, just a little. "Then maybe the other girls won't want it either."

"They're all like Tara!" Wanda said. "We'll never be able to win against all of them! They're all spoiled and conceited and snobby and mean! They're all—"

"Whoa there, Wanda Wilson!" Cheree said again. "That girl Beth Ann seemed okay to me."

"Beth Ann?" Wanda said.

"Sure," Wanda said. "She seemed friendly enough. I don't think she much likes being bossed around by Tara Bradwell either."

Now that she thought about it, Wanda saw that Cheree was right; Beth Ann *did* seem to be okay. Maybe she and Wanda wouldn't have to take on Tara all by themselves after all!

She reached up and took the other side of Clancy's bridle, urging the horse forward and hurrying Cheree along with him. "Come on," she said, "we don't have much time before my classes start."

"Where are we goin'?"

Wanda smiled. "I think it's time we *both* got to know the other girls in the riding club!" she said.

Chapter Seven

Tara Bradwell called all the members and asked them to come to an emergency meeting of the Apple Valley Riding Club at six-thirty Monday night. *Ordered* was more like it. "Be there!" she said.

The other nine members were in the club room waiting for Tara when she got there. Six of them were dressed in plaid flannel shirts, faded jeans, and Western hats in assorted sizes and colors. Cheree Davenport was sitting with them.

"Hey there, Tara Bradwell!" they said when she walked in the door.

Tara stood in the doorway, her mouth hanging open. It didn't take her long to see that she was outnumbered. Any resolution to make the club all-English would be voted down at least six to four—seven to four if they counted Cheree. Tara narrowed her eyes at Wanda, who was wearing Cheree's teal, lavender, and fuchsia cowgirl hat. It was a little too big for her and tended to slip down over her eyebrows. "You think you're pretty smart, don't you?" Tara said.

Wanda shook her head, setting the hat jiggling back and forth. "We just think Apple Valley should be a club for *all* riders."

"Fine!" Tara said. "You do whatever you want. I quit!" She stomped over to her display area and started pulling down her ribbons.

Beth Ann, who was the secretary of the Apple Valley Riding Club, came to the front of the room. "I guess we should hold a new election for president," she said. "We need somebody who is organized and dedicated."

"Somebody who is willing to put a lot of time into the club," another girl said.

"Somebody who can figure out what needs to be done and get people to do it," a third girl added.

"Okay," Beth Ann said. "The floor will take nominations."

Over at the side of the room, Tara Bradwell kept pulling down ribbons and stuffing them into a box.

Wanda fingered the silver cross that she was wearing on the *outside* of her flannel shirt. "I nominate Tara Bradwell," she said.

Tara froze, a blue ribbon dangling from her hand.

"I second the nomination," Cheree said.

Tara spun around and looked at them, her eyes wide with disbelief.

"I move the nominations be closed," Beth Ann said.

Tara wiped at her eyes with the back of her hand. "You don't want me," she said.

"Sure we do," Wanda told her. "Everybody talked about it already, before you got here. We all know you're organized and dedicated."

"And you give a lot of time to the club," Beth Ann added.

"And *everybody* says that nobody can tell people what to do or get them to do it like you," Cheree said. She laughed her contagious laugh, and everybody in the room joined in. Even Tara Bradwell.

The vote to keep Tara as president was unanimous. There was no other new business, so the meeting adjourned to the riding ring, where Cheree gave some of the other girls a chance to try their hand at maneuvering around a couple of flowerpots and garbage cans on Clancy. Nobody but Tara tried it at much more than a slow trot.

"Whoooee," Cheree teased. "I've never seen *slow-motion* barrel racing before!"

"Okay, smarty," Wanda told her. "Let's see you ride English."

Cheree was up to the challenge. She borrowed Gypsy and traded in her cowgirl hat for Wanda's riding cap.

The other girls giggled at her grunts and grimaces as she bent her long legs enough to stick her feet in the shortened English stirrups.

They hooted when she sat straight and stiff in the saddle, sucked in her cheeks to make her face look extra-serious, then flapped her knees and reins up and down to try to get Gypsy moving.

And they nearly rolled on the ground with laughter when she tried her version of English

58

posting, lifting herself in an exaggerated, out-of-rhythm motion, up and down, as Gypsy cantered when Cheree wanted her to trot, and walked when she wanted her to canter.

"I say," she said in a mock-English accent as an out-of-control Gypsy trotted her past the rail. "There's nothing to it!"

"You look like you're riding a trampoline!" Tara called out. She laughed cheerfully, and Cheree laughed right along with her.

After the lessons, Wanda and Cheree helped Tara put her ribbons back up on her display board. "Bring yours in next time, and I'll help you put them up," Tara told Cheree.

Later, when the other girls had gone home and Wanda and Cheree were in the boarding barn sharing an after-grooming snack with Clancy and Gypsy, Wanda laughed about Tara's offer. "She's just anxious to count them," she told Cheree.

"That's okay," Cheree said, grinning. "I'll be sure to bring in fewer than she has, to keep her happy."

Wanda was beginning to realize that she could learn a lot from Cheree Davenport, and most of it wasn't about horses or riding. "You'd do that, even after the way she acted toward you?" she said.

Cheree shrugged. "Turn the other cheek and all, you know. Besides, I'm not one for fightin' battles I can avoid," she said.

"Hey, that reminds me—I'm taking Gypsy on a trail ride on the Gettysburg Battlefield this weekend," Wanda told Cheree. "You and Clancy want to come along? We'll pack a lunch and give you the grand tour!"

"Whooee!" Cheree said. "That sounds like fun."

Gypsy nickered, and Clancy nodded his head as if they both agreed.

Don't miss these exciting stories in the Winners series . . .

Batter Up, Bailey Benson!

Bailey and Nicole are inseparable best friends, and they've been practicing hard for softball try-outs. But when they are put on different softball teams, instead of playing together, they are forced to compete—the Orioles' best pitcher against the White Sox's best batter.

Can Bailey and Nicole be rivals and best friends, too? What happens when Nikki plans to put the hotshot pitcher in her place in the upcoming Orioles-White Sox match-up? You might be surprised by the ending!

ISBN: 0-310-20705-3

Go Figure, Gabriella Grant!

Gabriella dreams of making it to the Olympics as a figure skater. But is all the hard work—and missing out on other activities—really worth it? Not only that, the latest sessions with her coach have gone badly. Will she be ready to compete in the regional qualifiers?

As much as Gabriella loves skating, she is starting to wish she could just quit.

Don't miss the outcome as Gabriella finds out what wonderful reason God has for giving Gabriella the talent of skating.

ISBN: 0-310-20702-9

Use Your Head, Molly Malone!

Molly talked her sister Sarah into joining the soccer team. She even taught Sarah the game! But when Sarah gets to play forward—the position Molly has hoped for—and Molly gets stuck playing fullback, Molly thinks it's not fair. Why should she have to play defense while Sarah gets to score all the points and get the attention from everyone?

But soccer games aren't won by star players. They're won by good teamwork. And Molly is about to learn this valuable lesson. Find out what happens when Molly and Sarah's team faces an opponent and defeat stares their team in the face.

ISBN: 0-310-20704-5

Whoa There, Wanda Wilson!

Wanda's dream came true when she became a member of the Apple Valley Riding Club. That is until the new girl, Cheree, showed up.

The newcomer is a great rider and a lot of fun, too, and Wanda finds it impossible not to like her— even though the president of the riding club, Tara, dislikes her because she's different. Cheree rides Western, but the Apple Valley Riding Club members ride English.

Wanda is angry with Tara and the other club members. After all, who are they to judge Cheree? But is everyone in the club guilty of wrongly judging others, or is Wanda? You'll find out when Tara sets out to bar Cheree from the Apple Valley Riding Club.

ISBN: 0-310-20703-7

ZondervanPublishingHouse

Grand Rapids, Michigan

A Division of HarperCollins*Publishers*

We want to hear from you. Please send your comments about
this book to us in care of the address below. Thank you.

ZondervanPublishingHouse
Grand Rapids, Michigan 49530
http://www.zondervan.com